TO _____

DISNEY'S
SMALL WORLD LIBRARY
LAPLAND FRIENDS
An Adventure in Sweden

GROLIER ENTERPRISES INC.
DANBURY, CONNECTICUT

© The Walt Disney Company. All rights reserved.
Printed in the United States of America.
Developed by The Walt Disney Company in conjunction with Nancy Hall, Inc.
ISBN: 0-7172-8218-X

"Sweden, at last!" Huey shouted gleefully.

"This will be a great vacation!" added Louie.
"Grandma Duck says we'll be able to ski every day near
Uncle Sven's and Aunt Gerta's house!"

The boys hurried off the plane at Arlanda Airport in
Stockholm and ran to greet the elderly couple waiting at
the bottom of the ramp.

"Such big boys!" said Aunt Gerta as she hugged the nephews.

"We can't wait to get to your house," said Louie.

"We have some time before our train leaves for the north," said Uncle Sven. "We thought you boys might enjoy seeing Stockholm."

"That sounds great!" said Dewey.

Uncle Sven and Aunt Gerta took the three boys to the dock, and everyone climbed aboard a sightseeing boat.

"The city of Stockholm is made up of 14 small islands," explained Uncle Sven. "All the islands are connected by bridges so people can travel by car and train."

"Look over there!" said Huey, pointing to a magnificent building.

"That's the Royal Palace," said Aunt Gerta. "This is where the King of Sweden works. It is also used for important meetings."

After the boat ride was over, Uncle Sven and Aunt Gerta led the boys to Central Station to catch their train.

They settled in their seats, and the train began to move. The city of Stockholm spread out beyond the windows.

The sight of flowers and green grass worried Louie. "It doesn't look like we'll be able to ski," he said sadly.

"Oh, yes, you will," said Aunt Gerta. "Up north there is snow until late spring and even summer."

"Sweden is a very large country," explained Uncle Sven. "The weather here in the south of Sweden is very different from the weather where we live, in the north."

"You boys have had a long trip," said Aunt Gerta. "Now it's time to get some rest. We still have quite a way to go."

When the boys woke up the next morning, they looked out of the train windows and saw beautiful forests and streams. Best of all, everything was covered with snow!

Later that day, the train slowed down. "Look!" said Aunt Gerta.

Huey, Dewey, and Louie saw a line of stones beside the train tracks. Next to the stones was a sign that said they were crossing the Arctic Circle.

"Wow!" said Huey. "We're at the North Pole!"

"Not quite," said Uncle Sven, chuckling. "But we are farther north than most people ever go."

The train finally stopped in a little snow-covered town.
"Hello!" said a man with a booming voice. "Now tell
me, who is Huey, who is Louie, and who is Dewey?"
Uncle Sven and Aunt Gerta introduced their friend
Carl to the boys. Carl had brought his snowmobile bus to
take them all to Uncle Sven's and Aunt Gerta's house
outside of town.

They climbed into the snow bus and drove off.

"What kind of sign is that?" asked Huey.

"That is a Moose Crossing sign," said Carl. "You'll see plenty of moose around here."

"And also reindeer," added Aunt Gerta. "We are in Lapland now, and many Lapps herd reindeer."

Sure enough, a few minutes later they saw a herd of reindeer crossing the road.

"I didn't know we were in Lapland," said Dewey in a puzzled voice. "I thought we were in Sweden."

Carl stopped the snow bus by a young boy who was tending the reindeer.

"I'd like you to meet Lanuk," said Carl. "He is a Lapp, and he can tell you all about Lapland."

"The northern part of Sweden is called Lapland," explained Lanuk. "Lapland also stretches across the northern parts of Norway and Finland, and even a small part of the Soviet Union."

Just then an old reindeer left the herd and came to nuzzle Lanuk's neck.

"Some of our reindeer are more like pets," he said, laughing. "My father gave me this reindeer when I was three years old. His name is White Horn."

"He seems really nice," said Louie. "I never knew anyone who had a reindeer for a pet before."

"White Horn is a wonderful pet," agreed Lanuk.

Then they all waved good-bye to Lanuk and drove on. Carl dropped them off at a little cottage at the top of a mountain.

The boys walked inside the house.

"That's the biggest stove I've ever seen!" said Huey when he entered the kitchen.

"It's a wood-burning stove," said Aunt Gerta. "Uncle Sven and I are the town bakers, so that stove gets plenty of use."

The next morning the boys had some delicious bread that Uncle Sven and Aunt Gerta had made. Then, they helped Uncle Sven load up a toboggan with boxes of bread and cakes to take down to the village. The boys skied and Sven walked on snowshoes while pulling the toboggan.

"Why don't you get a snow bus like Carl's to make your deliveries, Uncle Sven?" asked Dewey.

"Snow buses cost a lot of money," said Uncle Sven. "Besides, I'm getting old, and I'm not used to things that move so fast."

They had just finished the last delivery when they met
Lanuk. He was looking at a blouse in a store window.

"I've been saving money to buy that for my mother's
birthday," Lanuk explained.

Then he turned to the boys. "I was wondering if you
would like to come home with me and meet my family,"
said Lanuk.

Uncle Sven agreed to let the boys go, and they headed
off for Lanuk's settlement.

Lanuk brought the boys to his hut and introduced them to his mother. She was making a coat.

"Lapps can make almost anything," Lanuk said proudly. "We make boots, blankets, and even jewelry." He showed the boys a bracelet decorated with thin threads of tin.

"Lapps are famous for this kind of jewelry," added Lanuk's mother.

Lanuk led the boys outside to show them the rest of the settlement. He told them about the Lapp way of life.

"Some Lapps travel, or migrate, with the reindeer herds," he explained. "Other Lapps are farmers, lawyers, or professors, and they live in one place only. But my family still follows the reindeer."

Lanuk explained how reindeer dig under the snow to get at the moss growing there. "When the moss is gone, the herd must move on," Lanuk said.

Just then Lanuk's father came speeding along on a
snowmobile. "Time for dinner," he said, and the four boys
hopped aboard.

The snowmobile ride was even more fun than the
snow bus. In no time at all, they were back at Lanuk's
hut.

They all sat down on rugs before a low table. Lanuk's baby sister lay in a splendid cradle that Lanuk and his father had made for her.

"And my mother made the rugs we are sitting on," said Lanuk.

His mother nodded. "My grandmother taught me how to make rugs, clothing, and many other things," she said.

After dinner the three boys returned to Uncle Sven's and Aunt Gerta's house. There they found Uncle Sven asleep in a chair.

"Each time he takes the bread into town, he comes home exhausted," said Aunt Gerta in a worried voice. "I wish there were an easier way to make our deliveries."

When the boys went to bed that night, they tried to think of a way to help Uncle Sven and Aunt Gerta.

"Maybe Lanuk knows a good way to make the deliveries," said Huey. "Let's ask him tomorrow," agreed Dewey.

When they arrived at the Lapp settlement the next morning, most of the Lapps had packed their belongings.

"We are supposed to leave today on the migration," said Lanuk's father, "but we cannot find Lanuk."

"We'll help you look for him," said Dewey.

Thinking that Lanuk might have gone to buy his mother the blouse, the boys went to the village store. But Lanuk was not there.

The boys went to the snow-covered pasture where they had first met Lanuk, but the field was empty.

Then Huey saw something in the distance. "There's some smoke!" he exclaimed. "Maybe Lanuk is over there!"

The boys ran to the woods, where they found Lanuk crouched over a small fire keeping warm. White Horn was beside him.

"Lanuk!" cried Dewey. "We've been looking all over for you! You have to go home to begin the migration."

"I'm not going," declared Lanuk. "My father told me to leave White Horn behind because he is too old and slow and can't keep up with the herd. But I won't do it! White Horn and I will stay here by ourselves."

"I don't think your family will like that," said Louie.

"I won't leave White Horn here all by himself!" said Lanuk in a determined voice.

Suddenly Huey had an idea. "Suppose we buy White Horn from you," he said to Lanuk. "We can give White Horn to our aunt and uncle, and he can help them pull their toboggan into town. And then you'd have enough money to buy your mother that blouse."

"Best of all, White Horn will still be here when you get back in the fall," added Dewey.

Lanuk grinned and hugged White Horn. "That sounds like a wonderful idea!" he said.

"You are very kind to help me," said Lanuk. "I hope you will come back and visit Lapland again someday."

"Sure!" said the three boys. They said goodbye to Lanuk and went back to the house.

The elderly couple couldn't believe their eyes when they saw White Horn.

"This is a wonderful gift!" said Uncle Sven. "With White Horn to pull the toboggan, I won't have any trouble making our deliveries!"

When it was time for the boys to leave, White Horn
nuzzled them the way he had nuzzled Lanuk.

"We've really had some great times in Sweden," said
Louie.

"And we've made some good friends," said Huey.

"That's right," said Dewey. "And one of them even has
antlers!"

Did You Know...?

Every country has many different customs and places that make it special. Some of the things that make Sweden special are mentioned below. Do you recognize any of them from the story?

The part of Sweden that lies inside the arctic circle is known as the Land of the Midnight Sun. Here, during part of the summer, the sun never sets. People let down heavy blinds over their windows at night so they can sleep.

Stockholm, Sweden's capital city, is built on 14 islands that are linked by 50 bridges. Many Swedish people own pleasure boats, and they use them for vacationing and visiting friends.

The Lapps, who call themselves Saamis, live on land inside the arctic circle that is owned by several countries, including Sweden. They are among the smallest peoples in the world. Although Lapps average only five feet in height, they are very strong. Lapps wear colorful traditional costumes, including the Cap of the Four Winds. It has four floppy points and bright streamers that flutter in the wind.

Kiruna, Swedish Lapland's only city, is the largest city in the world—at least in area. This city has three times more land than the state of Rhode Island, but less than 30,000 people live there.

Sweden is a land of great natural beauty.
Half the country is covered with
green forests, and there are
thousands of lakes. Most Swedes
spend their summer vacations
at cottages on lakes or near
the sea.

Cross-country skiing is a national sport in
Sweden. In the most famous cross-country
race, skiers from around the world race a
long distance between two small towns.

Like many European countries,
Sweden has a royal family.
The king and queen of Sweden
live with their children in a
palace on an island outside
of Stockholm.

Early Swedish warriors, called Vikings, sailed the sea and explored new lands. Some Vikings probably sailed as far as North America, hundreds of years before Columbus.

Bread is an important food in Sweden. In early times, bread was baked only once a year and then stored on poles strung along the ceiling.

Many Lapps speak Swedish as well as their native Saaomi Language. Swedish and English are related languages with many words that are similar. Can you tell what these Swedish words mean? *Moder, fader, syster,* and *broder.*

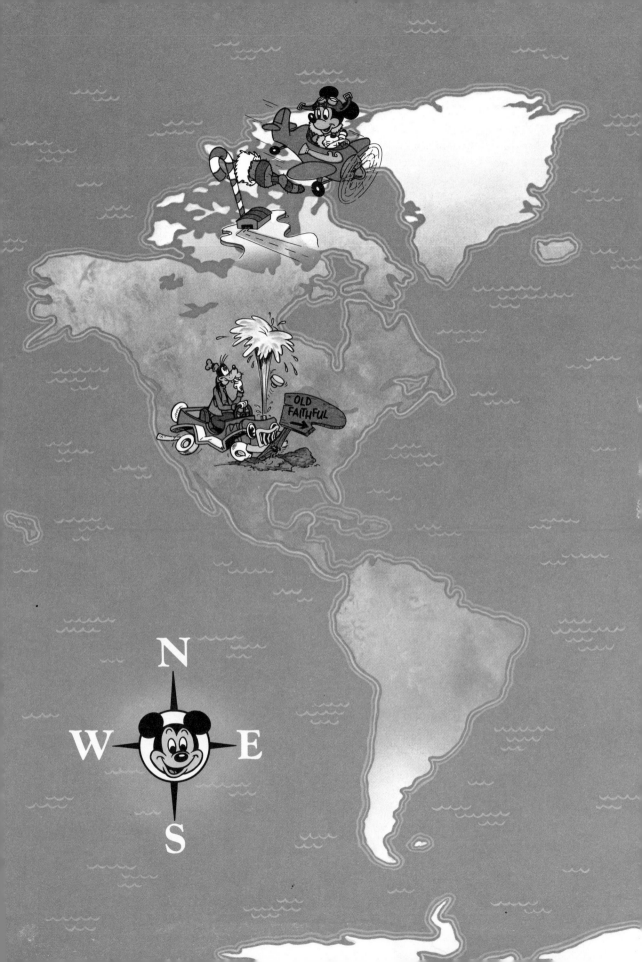